The Amazing Erik

To Becky Klay, who lets children discover the magic within
—Mike Huber

To my three amazing kids
—Joseph Cowman

Published by Redleaf Lane
An imprint of Redleaf Press
10 Yorkton Court
Saint Paul, MN 55117
www.RedleafLane.org

First edition 2014
Book jacket and interior page design by Jim Handrigan
Main body text set in Billy
Typeface provided by MyFonts

Manufactured in Canada
20 19 18 17 16 15 14 13   1 2 3 4 5 6 7 8

Library of Congress Control Number: 2013939329

The Amazing Erik

Written by
MIKE HUBER

Illustrated by
JOSEPH COWMAN

Redleaf Lane

Erik was playing at the water table.
He watched the blue water swirl down
the funnel and race through the tube.
It spilled into the yellow water. Like magic,
a green cloud appeared.

Erik poured more and more blue water until the yellow was a sea of green. He waved his hands and said,

"Airdah-taroo!"

"I could turn the whole world green," he thought.

Then he noticed his sleeve had unrolled into the water.

There were three things that always made Erik cry:
balloons popping, scary dreams, and wet sleeves.

And now his sleeve was soaked, so Erik began to cry.

Regina, his teacher, came over.
"What's wrong, Erik?" she asked.
Erik pulled on his wet sleeve.

Regina knelt down. "I can see you're sad," she said. "Your shirt's not *too* wet. It should dry quickly."

But Erik kept crying.

Regina said, "It sounds like you want a new shirt. I'll go get you one."

Regina stepped away, and Erik began to calm down. Then he saw that his shoe was wet too.

Now there were four things that made Erik cry.

Erik closed his eyes.
He wondered if he would
ever be able to stop crying.

When Erik opened his eyes, he saw Rita standing near him. She handed him a rag and smiled at him.

She plunged another rag into the water with a **SPLOOSH**.
She dropped the rag on the floor with a **SLOPP**.
"I'm cleaning the floor," Rita said.

Erik watched as the green water pooled around Rita's rag. Rita pushed the rag back and forth across the floor, spreading the green around. Rita said, "I'm the washer. You're the dryer."

Erik sniffed back his tears and said, "You really made the floor wet." He slid out of his chair and began to dry the floor. He wiped his rag back and forth, and it soaked up some of the water. "Like magic," Erik thought.

Erik held his rag up in the air and said, "The Amazing Erik will now make the water disappear."

He said to Rita, "You make the water appear. I'll make the water disappear. Like this." He waved his rag across the green and said, **"Airdah-taroo!"**

Rita smiled. She dropped her wet rag on the floor again, and some water splashed up on her skirt. **"Sloppity-sloo!"** she said.

There were many things that made Erik laugh, and Rita was at the top of the list. He started giggling. Rita giggled too. Soon they were laughing loudly together.

Just then, Regina reappeared with a dry shirt for Erik.

"Watch this, Regina!" Erik said. He waved his rag over some water, and it vanished from the floor. **"Airdah-taroo!"**

Regina smiled and said, "You don't seem sad anymore."

Erik sat up and thought. "I'm not sad," he said. "I'm happy. I'm playing magician with Rita." Erik smiled. "We're going to make the whole world turn green."

A Note to Readers

Sometimes young children become upset over small things. Take Erik, for example. He becomes upset when his shirtsleeve gets wet. Like Erik, most young children experience emotions very intensely. Each emotion, in the moment, is a big deal. Emotions can be overwhelming for young children because they don't know how to cope with or process their feelings. And when the emotion is a difficult one, like sadness, fear, or anger, it can feel as though the emotion they are experiencing will never go away.

When a child is upset, the best thing you can do is simply acknowledge the child's feelings. Ms. Regina does this when she says to Erik, "I can see you're sad," and reassures him that the shirt will dry. By acknowledging the emotion the child is feeling, you communicate, "I can see that you're upset, but I'm here with you now." And really, that's what matters most.

We hope *The Amazing Erik* shows children that while some emotions are upsetting, they won't last forever—especially when a caring adult is there to help.

—〰—

Erik's spinal injury affects his ability to walk. Although he needs a wheelchair, he is still able to get out of it by himself and sit on the floor. Children who use wheelchairs have varying challenges. Some children aren't able to get out of their wheelchairs unassisted.